To our parents... and to Patricia, Adriana, Guille, Pablo and Leo.
We love you, gang!

SILVIA y DAVID

To Javi, who has made this book grow with me, and to Tomeu,
for feeding our souls and bodies during its creation.

MERCÈ

Syncretic Press

Published by Syncretic Press, LLC.
PO Box 7401, Wilmington, Delaware 19803
www.syncreticpress.com
Direct all questions to info@syncreticpress.com

2021 by Syncretic Press, LLC – First edition in English
Hereafter, by Silvia and David Fernández
Text copyright © 2021 by Silvia and David Fernández
Illustrations copyright © 2021 by Mercè López
Translation by Marita Thomsen. Edited by Anna Wood
ISBN: 978-1-946071-31-6
Library of Congress Control Number: 2020934567

Translation of *Más allá*. First published in Spain
Copyright © 2017 by Pastel de Luna
Text copyright © 2017 by Silvia and David Fernández
Illustrations copyright © 2017 by Mercè López

Printed in China

Syncretic Press

HEREAFTER

SILVIA AND DAVID FERNÁNDEZ

MERCÈ LÓPEZ

Syncretic Press

The artists of Galaxy Circus risk their lives every day –
jumping between trapezes without a net,
eating fire and swallowing swords, flying out of cannons...
That is probably why they talk so much about death,
wondering: What comes after this?
What will we experience in 'the hereafter'?

At Galaxy Circus there are as many different answers to these questions as there are fins, antennas and snouts.

Ángel Domingo, the *shark of the skies*,
believes that when we die...

... we go to Heaven, and there we will be reunited with our loved ones.

Juanito González, *the incredible canine cannonball...*

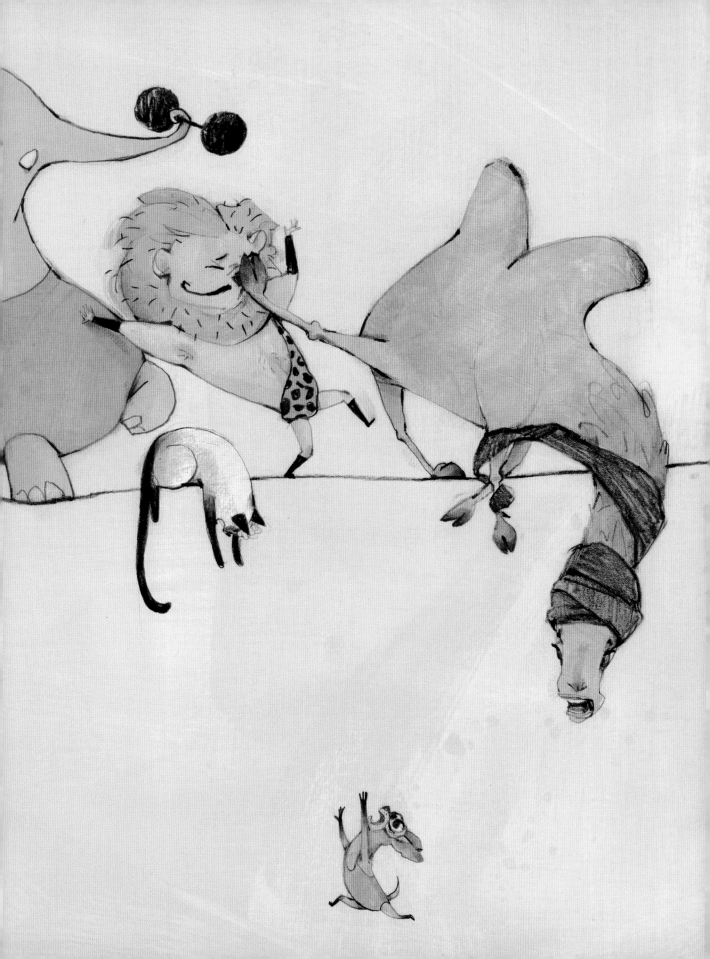

I JUST KNEW THIS WOULD HAPPEN.
</ Remy> :Fatal Error 1999-202?
BILLY WILDER
I'm a writer, but then nobody's perfect.
GROUCHO MARX
Excuse me, I can't stand up

... also thinks that we go straight to Heaven, but that sometimes, on certain days of the year, we come back to visit our friends and have big parties.

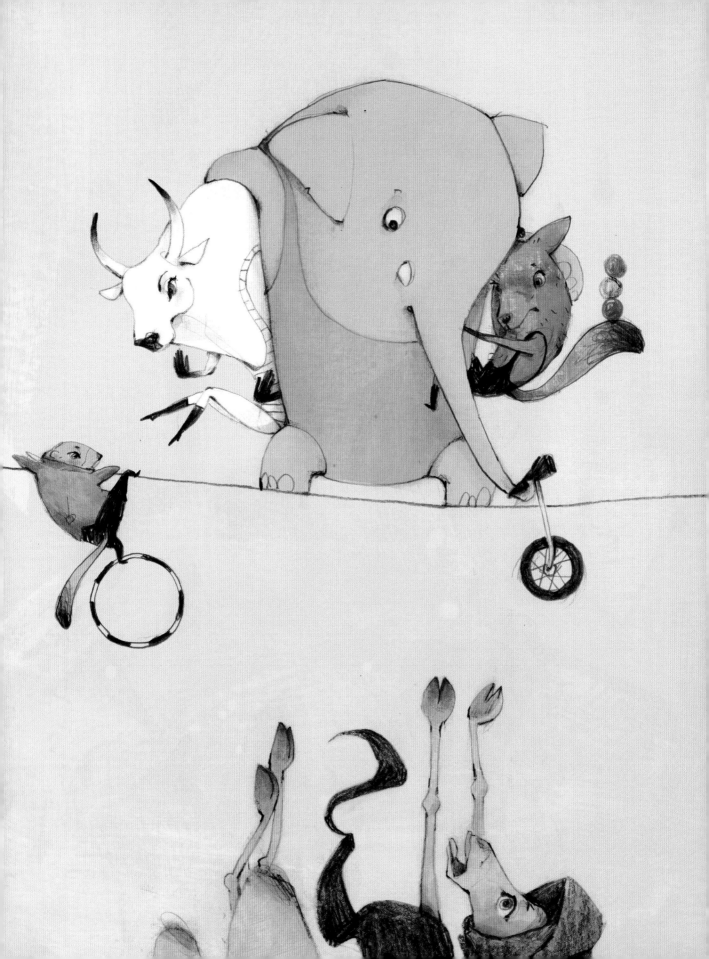

And what about Fatima...?

Fatima, *the enchantress of the desert*, believes that when we die, the Garden of Eden awaits us, an oasis of infinite wonders, rivers of milk and honey, and the daintiest delicacies.

Gerónimo, *the coyote of the prairies,*
thinks that when we die...

... we become spirits that can communicate
with the living through the four elements:
earth, wind, fire and water.

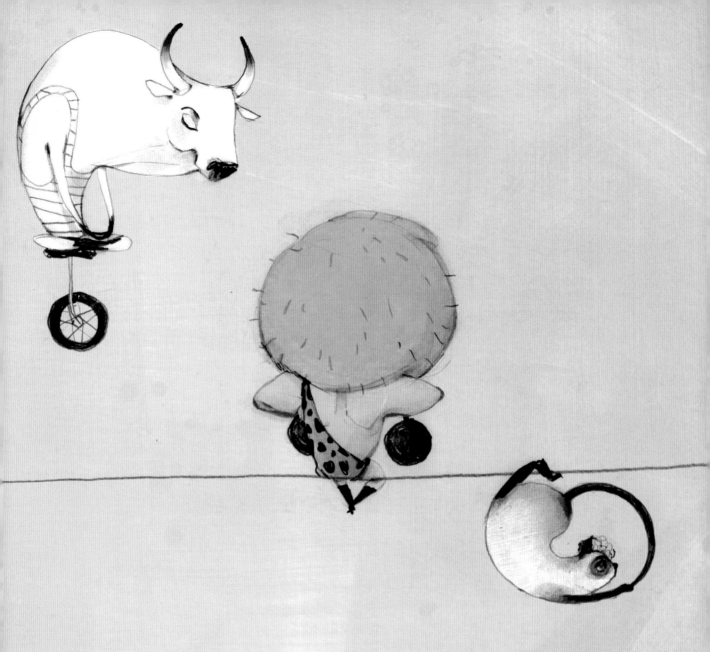

Ramses, *the freewheeling scarab...*

... believes that we will go on a thrilling journey full of adventures through the mysterious Realm of the Dead.

While Federica, *the fearless marmot...*

... is convinced that we will be born again and live our lives exactly the way we just have, again and again.

And again... And again... And again...

Pema Houdini, *the great escapist...*

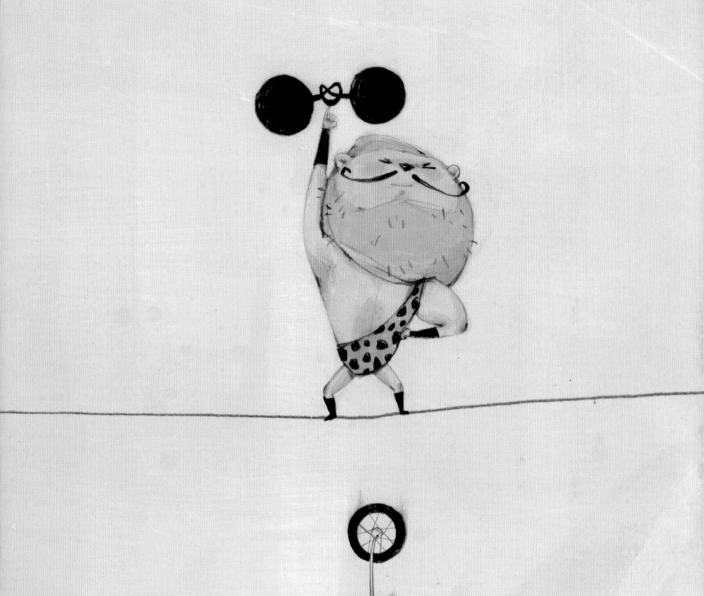

... also believes that we live many lives, but a different one each time, and reincarnated as different animals: we could become a cow, a mosquito, an ostrich...

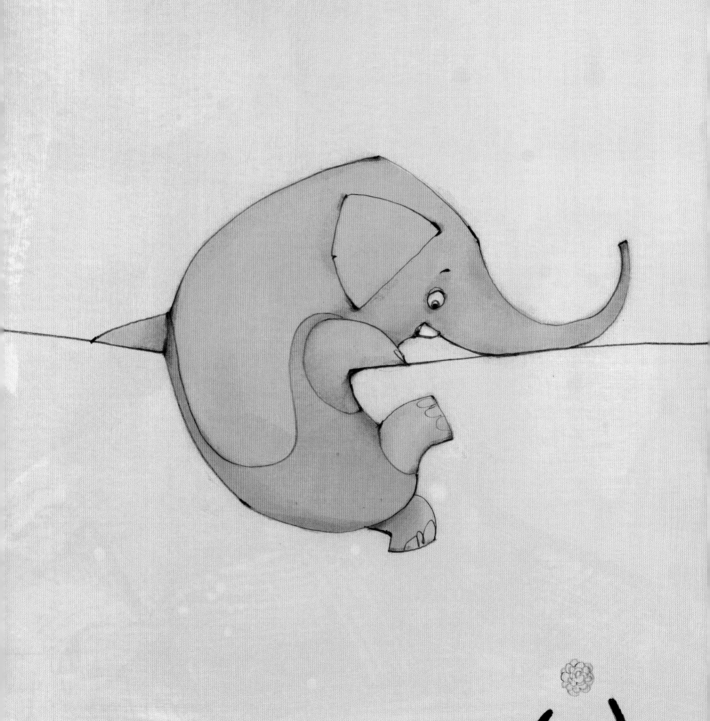

Frida, *the queen of the trapeze*,
is convinced that when we die...

... we live on in our creations and the memories of others.

Siddhartha, *the master of the tightrope...*

... hopes to reach Nirvana and become part of the cosmic light that holds all of the world's beings together.

Leo, *the lion of steel*, believes
that when we die...

... our energy shines on forever in the universe
among the other stars.

And you... what do you believe?

Silvia Fernández

Silvia was born in Madrid, Spain. She has a PhD in Social Psychology from the New School for Social Research, in New York. She is also a Certified Instructor at the Center for Compassion and Altruism Research and Education (CCARE) at Stanford University. She has carried out investigations where she explores death through cultures, empathy, compassion and the benefits of mindfulness in oncological contexts. She taught social psychology and training in empathy and emotional regulation at universities such as The New School, CUNY and Columbia University, and at the NGO The International Justice Project.
Hereafter is her first foray into the world of children's literature.

David Fernández

David is a Spanish author and publisher. He originally studied veterinary medicine and worked for a few years in a small veterinary clinic in El Escorial, Madrid. Then he realized that his true passion was the world of books. So, together with some friends, he founded Pastel de Luna, a publishing company focused on children's picture books. He is the author of three illustrated books: *¿Dónde está tu nube?*, *Malina Pies Fríos* and *Hereafter*. The latter, written with his sister Silvia, has been translated into several languages.

Mercè López

Mercè was born in Barcelona. At the age of 11, she began oil painting and artistic drawing, later specializing in illustration at the Llotja School, in Barcelona.
Currently, she is involved in multiple activities, including graphic design, news media, cinema and theater, although her main focus is illustrating books. She has published more than 40 titles across Spain, France, the U.S. and Mexico.
In 2016, her work was part of the Seventh Hispanic-American Illustration Catalog. The following year, she was a representative of Catalonia in the collective exhibition Sharing A Future, at the Bologna International Children's Book Fair.

Other titles by

Syncretic Press

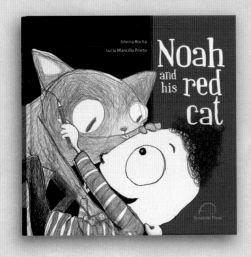

Noah and his red cat

Spanish Tortilla

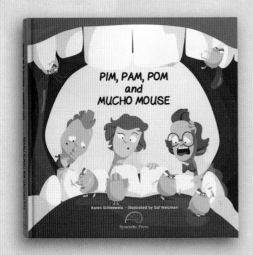

Pim, Pam, Pom and Mucho Mouse

Time to play

And many more at
www.syncreticpress.com